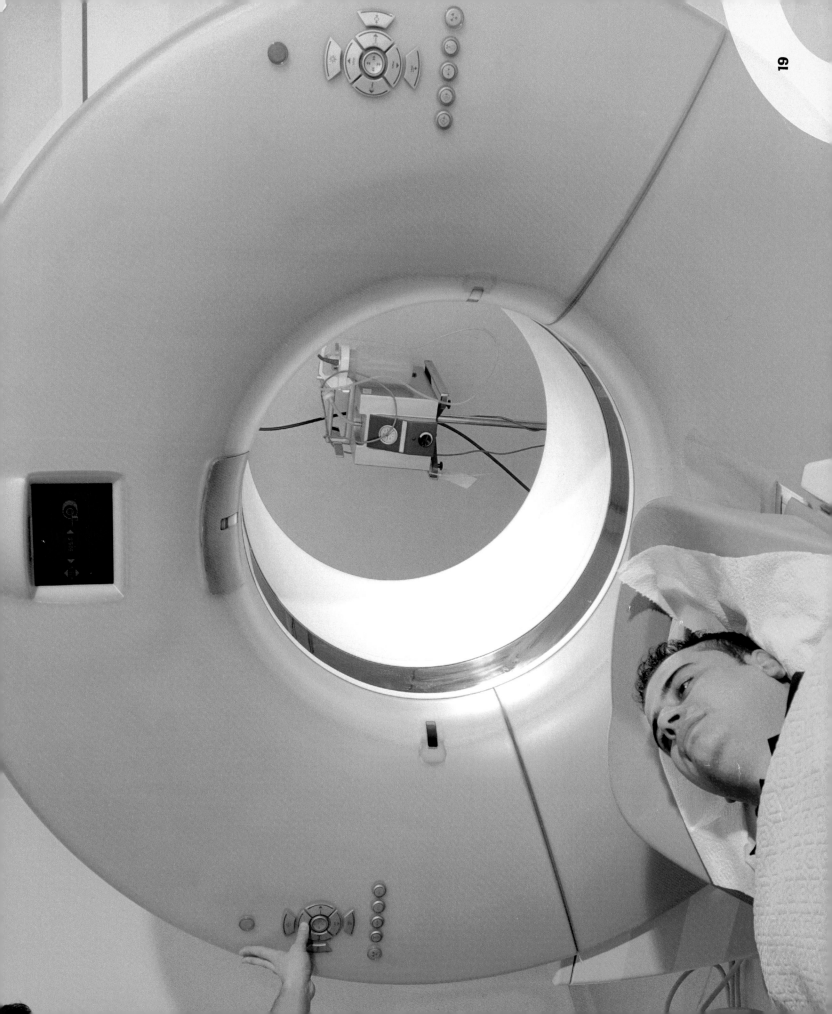

Magnets hold up pictures on
a refrigerator. Credit cards use
magnets to pay for what you buy.
Magnets are at work
everywhere you look!

Glossary

attract—to pull toward something

compass—an instrument used for finding directions

credit card—a small, plastic card used to pay for things; **credit cards** have a magnetic stripe on the back

energy—the ability to do work, such as move things

filing—a small piece that has been rubbed off of a larger piece

magnetic field—the area around a magnet that has the power to **attract** magnetic metals

MRI machine—a machine that uses a large ring magnet to make images of the inside of a person's body; **MRI** stands for magnetic resonance imaging

pole—one of the two ends of a magnet; a pole can also be the top or bottom part of a planet

repel—to push apart; like poles of magnets repel each other

Read More

McGregor, Harriet. *Magnets and Springs. Sherlock Bones Looks at Physical Science.* New York: Windmill Books, 2011.

Royston, Angela. *Magnets. My World of Science.* Chicago: Heinemann Library, 2008.

Vogel, Julia. *Push and Pull! Learn about Magnets.* Mankato, Minn.: Child's World, 2011.

Internet Sites

FactHound offers a safe, fun way to find Internet sites related to this book. All of the sites on FactHound have been researched by our staff.

Here's all you do:

Visit www.facthound.com

Type in this code: 9781429660693

Index

Word Count: 192
Grade: 1
Early-Intervention Level: 22

"That's a nice nest," said Duck.
"Yes, it is," said Chicken. "And I wouldn't swap it for *any*thing!"

Finally, she took the walking stick to Scarecrow. With a grateful sigh of relief, he leaned his tired old arms on the stick and gladly swapped it for his battered old hat.

Chicken took the hat and filled it with fresh, sweet-smelling straw….

She took the ribbon to Badger—
who swapped it for his walking stick.

She took the wool to Crow—
who swapped it for her ribbon.

She took the glasses to Sheep—
who swapped them for her wool.

Chicken took the blanket to Owl—
who swapped it for his glasses (the old ones, of course).

Donkey was delighted and, true to his word, swapped his blanket for the feathers.

Quick as a flash, Chicken pulled out one, two, three of her longest feathers and tied them to Donkey's tail.

"That's a nice blanket," said Chicken to Donkey.

"Yes, it is," replied Donkey. "But I'd rather have a few feathers. The flies drive me crazy, buzzing around my ears. My tail isn't quite long enough to flick them away. But if I had some long feathers tied to the end of it, I could swat them easily. I'd swap my blanket for a few long feathers any day."

"That's a nice pair of glasses," said Chicken to Owl.

"Yes, it is," said Owl. "My old ones broke, so I had to get a new pair. But I'd rather have a blanket. The sun streams through my window and keeps me awake all day, which wouldn't matter if I had a good, thick blanket to sleep under. I'd swap my glasses for a blanket any day."

Now Chicken didn't have a blanket, but she knew someone who did.

"That's a nice wool coat," said Chicken to Sheep.

"Yes, it is," replied Sheep. "But I'd rather have a pair of glasses. I have to keep a lookout for the wolf, and my eyes are not as good as they used to be. I really need a pair of glasses. I'd swap some of my wool for a pair of glasses any day."

Now Chicken didn't have a pair of glasses, but she knew someone who did.

"That's a nice ribbon," said Chicken to Crow.

"Yes, it is," said Crow. "But I'd rather have some wool. My nest is on this high, stone ledge, and it's very hard to sit on. I'd love some warm, soft wool to line it with. I'd swap this ribbon for some wool any day."

Now Chicken didn't have any wool, but she knew someone who did.

"That's a nice walking stick," said Chicken to Badger.

"Yes, it is," replied Badger. "But I'd rather have a piece of ribbon. It gets hot and stuffy underground, so I prop my door open with my stick. But I'm always tripping over it. If I had a ribbon, I could *tie* the door open. I'd swap my walking stick for a ribbon any day."

Now Chicken didn't have a ribbon, but she knew someone who did.

"That's a nice hat," said Chicken to Scarecrow.

"Yes, it is," replied Scarecrow. "But I'd rather have a walking stick. I've been standing here for years now, and my arms are so tired. I'd love a walking stick to lean on. I'd swap my hat for a walking stick any day."

Now Chicken didn't have a walking stick, but she knew someone who did.

The Scarecrow's Hat

Written and Illustrated by
Ken Brown

SCHOLASTIC INC.

New York Toronto London Auckland Sydney
Mexico City New Delhi Hong Kong Buenos Aires

For Ruth

ISBN 0-439-46509-5

Text and illustrations copyright © 2001 by Ken Brown. All rights reserved. Published by Scholastic Inc.,
557 Broadway, New York, NY 10012, by arrangement with Peachtree Publishers, Ltd. SCHOLASTIC
and associated logos are trademarks and/or registered trademarks of Scholastic Inc.

12 11 10 9 8 7 6 5 4 3 2 1   2 3 4 5 6 7/0

Printed in the U.S.A.   14

First Scholastic printing, September 2002

The Scarecrow's Hat